3 Jan 2016 — black eyed Poetry

Championship Evenings

In King's Head pub
until dawn found us
with a headless lamp
smashed on a wall,
the strewn floor:
a shirt, a sock, a shoe;
legs and arms wound
around a mannikan.

The sun finds us
a piece of everything.
Strange remnants
on this morning's shore,
thoughts we shook off
as a band played and
like the street last night
followed us home.

Championship Evenings

In King's Head pub
until dawn found us
with a headless lamp
smashed on a wall,
the strewn floor:
a shirt, a sock, a shoe;
legs and arms wound
around a mannikan.

The sun finds us
a piece of everything.
Strange remnants
on this morning's shore,
thoughts we shook off
as a band played and
like the street last night
followed us home.

For Cholpon and Sholah

Cat in the Sun Books
Part of the Redux Consortium
Binghamton, NY

Design: Brian Kasymaliev
Layout: Angela Mark
Publisher: Joe Weil
Editor: Emily Vogel
Consulting Editor: Micah Towery

ISBN: 978-1-946606-02-0

whwhwho fell out of that disordered Rainbow to the ground
My sisters were
Never were not the pleiades though they pled and
all the time for crayons and candy and mercy and time true
there's a million kilometers of concrete and rebar on the way down
to chicago or paradise or whatever else you have in mind
the fourth age the first days the last outposts of every
imagined heaven Nat'l GeoGraphic has mapped, photographed
illustrated monitered By the NSA NeGAradlized By Navy seals
in the pit of your heart in the frozen grocery aisle in upstate
New York and you know grief is only weakness like the twins at home
when Nancy told Margaret she was leaving and Margaret gasped "you
can't. she wont let you."

Table of Contents

Preparations to a Descent

You found me. It is the hour of not in the year of zero. Poured into a broken-down farmhouse of a hot, empty summer. There's no dawn for a few hours although it would seem little difference to mark. There's a book of geography on my desk lit up under a reptilian necked lamp. Or maybe it's the onion skinned brick of *Masterpieces of Modern Literature* that I stole from a teacher's desk that lies dead in front of me. There is another on geometry and another on biology, practical sciences I can't seem to get down no matter how much I want to be a scientist. I can't imagine how this place may have appeared when it was newly built. I have no guess as to when the house was built or what the first people may have looked like who lived in it, the shadows of their voices and movements are imagined and the whole of it lost. The room is ragged, the look of a bad hotel with bare patches of plaster where wallpaper tore away and green leaved linoleum that is chewed at the edges. The house trembles and cracks in a strong wind. There's a faint sour smell in the room like wet dog fur and cigars that is oddly restful. There is one tall window opened halfway to hear an easy rain hiss down into the dark lawn. My father is sleeping in the next room upstairs apart from my mother. I think I hear his rough breathing.

I woke up a moment ago and now sit beside the desk where at first I felt like I had a grand project to begin. That feeling passed and now it is only me in the hollow light smelling the words on a page, wanting to melt inside them. I'm uneasy and alone in this. I have yet to find my mouth and a mind that will attempt to draw these lines you read. I loved grief and anger too much because they felt like power and it corrupted all my knowing. I will learn this but it will not release me from the habit. I would see and taste and speak, but even now the page is artifact and the hour has collapsed. Maybe it's a poor conceit that wants when you read this testament, to summon me, but you are my ground of being now. I have no lineage, no spiritual ordinance.

I'm asking for yours.

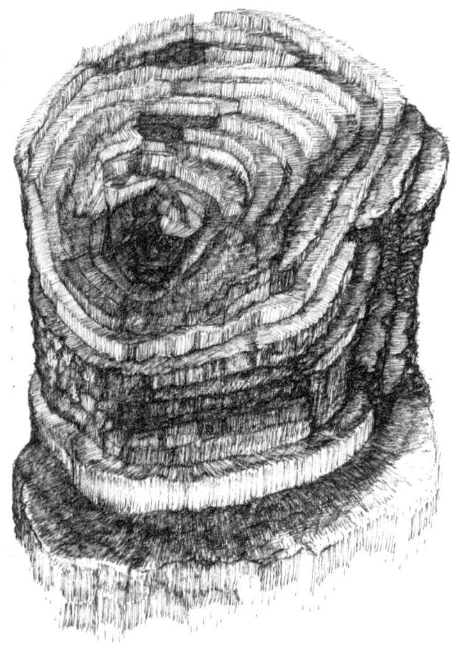

What You're In For

And beside the break
  in the window cut

  with stars, a lamp
      dumps light onto the floor,

a glass I forgot to put up
      spilled across the dining table.

Step off tonight,

  play that ruined Schumann again,
      needle skidding off the groove.

Go on, tell them what you saw
  outside in the safe dark:

      a bewildered field, a broken plank
in the wet grass, the brutal
  eloquence of things

  as they are
      unhelped.

Goodbye Friday

Where is my companion, my life in the world? Nothing sticks with me now. Like Krusoe in Brooklyn, the way they laugh at my pants made of sticks and my coconut hat. I'll shut up. Allow me one shout before all the good past dead loved friends I can't talk to anymore, hang my name in rattled newspapers on kiosk racks, before my undiscovered life appears somewhere else. I miss the sanctuary islands, the sky pouring in on the beach, fresh morning sea, bright sulfur mist strung with the wheeling cries of gulls, and I can only imagine if I'm ever going to get it right again. It's all strangers and judges here. I won't have the methodology or the supplier to replace my former life. Talking myself on the sand near a splintered pier that kind of half idea of a bridge extended to an ending in empty sky. And who am I now? Damn! Too soon too late. In all my affected armor, see inside my soul's kitchen where a boy is flogged by an illiterate mother because he can't find his good shoes for school.

Pisces

—maybe, spare light through the window helps illuminate the struggle against
annihilation … now maybe I'd like to have had that childhood in the Rhône-Alpes instead of
down in gullied Indiana backroads. I altogether love you even after you rub yourself off
on the furrow of someone's heart in that Chicago borough. I make rain

haunted sketches of Wicker Park … precious story … wasn't like you needed a brother
… sun and snow again. By now you know I'm ripping myself off … cologne dangling in
warm foyers of your mother's house on New Year's Day … candelabra dripping ice,
lowering itself as you walk in. When you never call, I wait … yo la tengo filtering

downstairs … torn photographs, half-cooked supper… speared roses into the icy lake.
That helpless sadness of a courtier poet who thinks he's Mister Big … an engagement ring
drowns in the Chicago river while behind me a pickup game cooks. I gave you a metal box with
twin fish enameled on the lid … spent all summer smithing. At the lake's split

bleached rocks, I wish I had it back, hadn't told you about the bullet through my sister's
kitchen window, hadn't ended with my hands shoved in my pockets, only this … kicking
stone … sweet red weather … voltaic splash … someone driving the outer lane … hard …

The Boy Who Was Christmas

They get me down
at Sixes and Central
making rounds.

Outside the lit air
is meat and potatoes.
Trade going down
in the alley we beg
for mercies and
miracle product
we once deserved.

A couple rolls
my niche of street.
I am where I am,
supper for two—
no truth like
the present to pay for.
Lean in tight. Ask,

"Who's the lucky fella tonight?"

Vintage Evenings

In a town no one cares to live,
the horns of cars swell
the wooded strand by a highway,

scare a deer across a river
run down against the dark

smalltown ball field,
where a drunk braves
the wet chill, grunts

stones out of the park
with a tennis racket,

the sound of someone
clearing a far wall.

Winter Hunger

Touch the track, a gash gnawed
in a branch. It's almost science.
Study a mood: a twisted weed
in remotes of a wood. Wait there
in the mud slog, in a rough blind,
where earth smells smoke and ice,
the feeling of alone in the middle
of the world where you can read
rain ticking cracked leaves from
the least scuttle of a hoof.
Dressed: cut the heft in clean strokes.
Don't forget the liver and heart.

River Daughter

I

In the faraway wood, my daughter and I bungee the floor tarp up
to let the rain flow under. Once shelter was made, I taught her

about building a fire with soaked wood. I snapped the neck of a branch
and it broke dry inside. With a hatchet I shaved the bark to dry wood underneath.

I used the knife to split it on a stump root. Tinder built to larger fuel.
The greasy feeling bark dried and cooked away. We slept inside our warm myth.

II

I heard an anguished pack of dogs swirl
in around our camp and away. I found
nothing in the morning but scuffled ground.
I had the worst dream.

Was this the purpose all along?

She was rain and swam away,
loosed on a tide. There. A semi pulling over,
opening for her, headlights her body's lantern
walking upright in the curved arm of a wave
of rain, her bare feet effortless, bend the thorns
along a dissolving road toward strange cities,
the almost world of men.

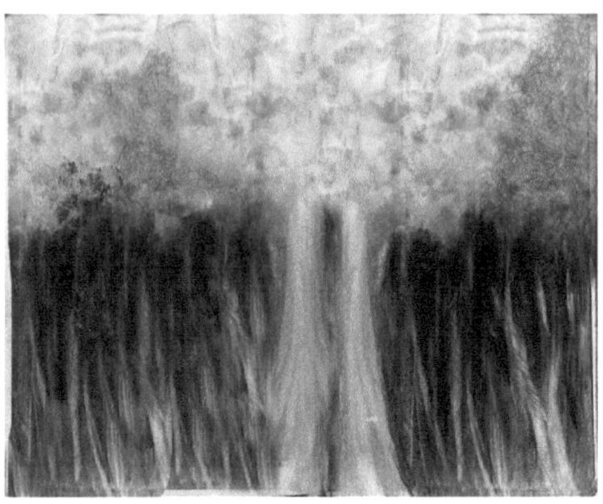

Her Hymn

My father works nights
digging for gold in Mexico.

In his unmade map
there is only winter,
only dirt.

After work, he brings home
fried fish in a paper bag
and beer from a tavern.

Sometimes I meet him
at the door. Mostly
I hide inside the low hours

where a blind rain runs
around the cracked planks

shacked together like
an overturned boat hull.

In an alley at the end

of the world,
no sound no

nothing clung to me
but the thick chunk
of a shovel in caked soil,

the lost cries of bone pottery,
poor fortunes in the earth.

He comes to the shirted lamp,
stands over my bed, his face

deep and fierce as Christ, dangling
salvation in his broken arms.

rednofive

You come here wanting,
off the Grand Blue Line,

pole dark in the middle
of ancient Chicago, outside
Red Number Five, a club

you were told she'd be
one last summer night. Now

looking to find her,
you don't want to look
and falter, disappoint yourself

if the blaze of cold breath
discharges on the street.

City rise shudders
wet and black, hangs
from a lazy spiral rain.

You'd like to climb inside,

so you can see her, see
grief surprises her and you
among faces lined to a door

where you're about to be turned out
on the street for a fake ID and,

since time and again, the armed
door won't open no matter
how much you lean into it,

force it to give.

Second Interview

The sun punches in a mirror, and it's enough,
Seeing ourselves again, beside a blue curtain,
Aligning a razor, adjusting the collar and cuffs;
As if it's all comes to this belated world,

This stiff puncture of a button through a fresh shirt.
Yet I forget where elsewhere subsided
To here as good as any other world,
Its mouthful of want, cold and muddy violets.

Spring shunts a series of lives missed, merging—
Circa you and me, repeating stay, sustain
In an emptied room, the extant universe,
Where I'm uneasy letting down a suitcase.

Lying in the mirror on a bed behind me,
She isn't sleeping beneath her unopened eyes.
But, slipping to her feet, approaching, her hands
Reach up around me and straighten my awkward tie.

She's asking, "can we go back to New Mexico?"

No. She's pulsating between shadow and sharp light,
Sudden glissando from inside, from an aching radio.
It's a simple attempt, wanting it right,

Wanting to save somewhere a day, a view
Pushing our limp ghost from room

To room in the belief, this time, this minute,

We might have it down. We might be endless.

Expelled

After I get fired
from the box factory, everything
is evidence— quick birds
        shoot the view

of a length of barbed wire and goldenrod
        struggling in gravel.

        I sleep in all summer,
carry laundry to the cleaners,

wait for it in cool passages
        where there's

a novel about the sea
        and refuge

from strangers asking

what are you
        looking at?

I'll bookmark myself, private

inside my going and coming
away from the anonymous
        messed up slag of buildings,

over there, where

I'd like to catch and tame
        a bird—

ask it what it is

to exist
        nameless
immediate

Traces of the Western Slopes

My grandfather's only known photograph
is a tintype flashed in the sear air under
Balancing Rock, Colorado. A stagecraft
carpenter, he travels the backs of maps.
On the rock, he's easy on horseback, leaning
the pommel, his face cast in a Gary Cooper
High Noon stoic. Near him, a young woman
on a mount, tacit in straight jet hair, sombrero.

My father never said. I had to ask,
though I felt I had no right to know
what guises his father wore.
When my father gives in he tells
a half-joke with no laugh in it,
says his father was a quiet bastard,
chief of police in league with bootleg
and the mayor's bordello, his name

expunged from the record books.
I want to ask if his father traced a necklace
of burnt mining towns from Baghdad
to Trinidad, the salt shore, an old river's
indirection. He won't say. Not how he died
or where his body is buried, or even that he vanished to air.
That hush brings me to the western edge.
I tell myself he must have watched waves flex

out and in, the west's afflictions, the Pacific
a squeezed press, that neither knows nor asks.
I lost it somewhere. Even a postcard
with yellow roses he penciled a trellis on,
the scribble to my grandmother Pearl:
"Put them on a string for me"—

Minor nfractions

I’d almost distill the rumor of her,
everything that got said about her,
to her crossed arms at the board,
refusing to do the solution.

Black eyed, she looked a fist.

She made pictures of her
boyfriend fucking her,
          and hung them in art class,

blazed joints at 2 a.m., cross-legged
in the middle of the soccer field,

her face stopped, cool, serene,
like she heard the rumored hallways,

was listening in on every distance:
a rattled trestle, summer pulsing

sharp in the dampening grasses,
the moon’s dragged muddy dress

over a tumble of trees and fields,
clouds bloated in a sort of rapture,

the awful thing it is, grown in the body,
a book report on the lives,
the figures I was never good at.

Morning Watch

Sweet coffee and oranges
—like they said after
that morning mercy eluded us.
The table kept its lines clean and quiet,
red and white squares.
It restates ideas of order,
a game's tacit rules you knew
because played over and over,
the play grew predictable as
days in rows or Sunday news
politely folded beside a plate
with sunny eggs and bacon.
The spoon with a fork
at rest in careful place near
evenly spaced salt and pepper,
the cream in such easy reach
that it feels predestined—
a vase's bright yellow burst
above a single table setting
knows how the sun works and
ruby throated birds in the garden
light us up in the mornings.
A Walther grips so good.
It belongs in your hand.

Consider a Move

No one ever lived here in the cold
translations of sunlight swollen
with smoke and rain among faceless
houses. Near buildings turn to cracked
chess pieces, a sign leans defaced.

Over the idle car beside the new and used.
Sunday empties into traffic lanes,
where its traffic lamps discover no one.
November sets up its shop of disrepair
in the stripped sky, vacant as a runway
for celestial chariots. In my own dark familiar—

Look, I'm no good at this and in truth,

I'm trying not to become the sum
of my fuckups. This flightless

story makes a poor craft,
a game of Go without stones, yet

one dream or another, some other city,

a late and secret twist of road. Look,
I wear myself out in the moment, leaving
this room I come back to, all tenor
and no vehicle to carry
me to where you are sleeping
with that prick, who can see you move
across a room to get a glass of water.

And there's me. Asking for a drink.

Asking For It

In the lair of the church basement,
        tiny chairs hug the table.

I walk the children's room
        where they fingerpaint and cut,
avoid the Jesus in his milky skin,
        his Shepherd's crook, rapping fist at a door;

his head's a tender conclude—like he's asking
        you to come up and kiss him—overhead, an organ groans.
My brother once asks why take us.
        We're going to hell in a coal chute anyway. Why not?

Why not ask a door to be more than door,
        do more than open to another
room I won't comprehend. Ask finally,

after the incensed homily subsides,
        and the Holy Ghost decamps, for merciful
triune ice cream, until Papa reaches us
        with the studied back of his hand,
strafes his wife— "you can't control
        your goddamn children."

Threnody

I ran the freak snowfall
	across the shaved lawns
of the funeral home

to the nursing home whose fire chute
	juts its mute windpipe

out of the wall. I ran
	from Jefferson to Monk's Lounge,
	the Baptist temple,
where the day slid off the face
	of the blushed dead brick

Safeway until it drained
	from the facets of cracked
glass lots completely. Against it,

I saw the mulatto
	girl walk the evening street

barefoot with a drink in her hand.
	Ice chuckled and she smiled
with an ankle bracelet. Sometimes
	I thought her dress,

it's made of gold coins,
	like her body is.

Then I got home and my father
	cried again and made me clean
the house. After supper the sink steamed

the kitchen window. A cold chime
	tingled off a hook
over the concrete porch next door.
	I watched a greasy bubble slip

up the air, lubricated with suds,
	heard the girl's pale violin upstairs
like bed springs. Her old man or mine.
	I can't believe

	the way they feed on us.

Air and Angle

I don't know how I get up there:
top of the stair, a dirty window's
drawn stare inhaling me as I

float down backwards to the bottom
of the stairwell, watch myself disappear
through a door, the small bulge
my hand makes fixed in hers.

I don't know how many times
we've done this though it feels

she's always led me to the dining table
where I'm up on my knees in a vinyl chair.

I see her through keyholes,
approaching hushed and cautious
as an animal stepping across a wood
bedded with crisp leaves.

A slash of hair hides her eyes.
She's narrow, in a straight dress
of no color I can recall.
She asks, "Want to see what I've got?"

The wings of her arms close in.
A bruised wallet opens from her hands,
spreads a fan of money from its fold,
smelling rich as skin. I'm bent in,

shaken inside out. My shirt lifts
a cotton fog over my face I can't see through.

Drivethru

The sun pulls up to the drive thru.
and in the scattered empty tables
a woman, maybe thirty, sits at the edge
of what may have once been a good idea.

Little crowns of paper tumble,
a car radio blasts horny country over
greased asphalt. She offers her ecstatic blue
tattoo, one more fleur di lis, Mitsubishi logo.

She's always waiting here,
blonde, bare midriff, her low slung pants
as before, as everything has to be
on the local meridian, on the bonework town,
on the bare horizon of her lemon yellow panty.

The rude building looks ill, squat
under a looming supermarket.
Her shadows drop down around her,

into the wet plastered newspapers singing
the first news of springtime under her feet:
dull fact of death, the usual sort of truth
and felony in our glands, bright pink helium
dripping in our mouths, in our hands.

Ascent

I lost an argument that night, stole a cigarette,
drank half a magnum of Merlot searching
for a coat to make into a pillow to sleep.
I'm not sorry I wanted to touch
the hem of her dress as if it could fly me
off the earth through an opening window.

In drunken sleep, dawn approaches.
I wish I were Ariel, New Year's night,
scaling the yew outside her apartment, risen
into the 3 am in three inch heels, who gashed
a cruel alphabet into the warped rungs

trying to get the moon, yelling into clouds
like clouds of birds circling in swirled waves,

her up stretched arm tilted to heaven,
crying the name of a Buryat sky god:

Aya Aya Aya

Restorations

How many times has the sky broken in on us?
Fled out of our hands like a draining balloon?
Of course, the moon looking through it
Is just the moon, full of itself, translucent as a voice.
Only the wind out of breath and unable
To quit prying at the one story house completely
Recalls the shape of where we lived instead.
There's no light working, yet everything works
Against it, the blue peeling back to dirty white.

For days the rain seeps in and weakens the walls,
It's still the house where I learned the word *moiety*.
The house all to pieces, repossessed by the solace
Of earth and grass, has it easy.
Because I've stood here every evening for a year,
Reworking memory into a small warm room
And on the solid, safe floor is my daughter,
Her life spread in liquetex and radiant ink, spattered
Across the clarity of a fresh sheet of paper.

Shone

It takes an hour for the bus to happen.

There's time to get my shit together,
throw the hamburger wrappers
and half-drunk milkshake away.
The sky hangs to the edges,
buildings thrown against the street
where cars sit dulled, wet.

Over Blessing's saxophone shop
little birds gang wires above a one story
brick factory with its papered windows.
Under the fog, crows dig precious scrap
out of numb snow. I'm glad for one day
bright enough to see through.

Far ahead of me a dark bulk
in the shape of a man turns
a corner and stares back.
No one believes these lives—
an overdue bill, a spiral fracture;
a time when the layered past
appears as though it's new.

Once, I walked to a pond sunk in woods,
it must have been in the last century,
far from the house where my family lived.
Rain turned inside itself, the sun moved
through it, sky broke loose for a moment
from clouds—I looked down. Something,
struggling in purpled leaves clutched in mud.
I stand in a frozen sky, fields rolled with wind—
a page on photosynthesis in my head,
a heat in the raised print my fingertips
lifted from the softcover Metamorphosis
writhing with gods, stolen from a teacher's desk.

My body rang and shone.

Dr. K Plays the Penguin Room

Whiskey swims the room

doctor bends a microphone
        strangled with a heart shaped thong.

Off stage, one or two hands clap,
New York pulsates—it's cold. Static charge

on cracked ice lamps and hydrants.
        The wind, the crowded murmur
moves around like a voice in a great room
that can't get out, throws

fits of snow bright in black reflections.

from the stage's cliff,
he winds his guitar
                his left hand

                drops the plectrum across
  the tropic dark, his Martin with Proust's face
glued on the body

                the facing flashes into the crowd.
his nomadic fingerprints press in.

        We feel them light as light
        all over our faces.

                We'd learn faith
                if we could believe it.

Comedy Hour

I listened too.

Learned I'm no nearer
the funny bone than I was.

Forty and I need a job,
improvising a yellow road

where a dog sleeps
off its wagged happiness.

Soaked in fog a hill holds
wicked trees full of crows:

folded hands in church.

If they knew to speak
do you think they'd live

as humans, work along
on the sketchy premises,

invite their friends in
for a laugh and music—

what would you call
laughter? A place

that doesn't exist beyond this page.

Mandelstam in the Corrective Labor Camp

At night the wall breathes stiff grunts.
His cot's unraveling sighs loosen

a rumor beneath the door of the investigation
of the Office of the Postmaster.

His mother writes, "You believe more in shadows
than what makes them."

He has a plastic mermaid in a dirty glass of water,
a book about frogs, a wrinkled periodical.

Spring's sick, climbs from the underground
smelling like tar and jasmine. Quick

climactic look of a world
at twilight, violet through locked

window grates. Private, hush. It's private.
When he talks, he ha ha ha's.

Water stutters out the taps
in rusty bursts. He looks for blood.

Above all, when he looks for a verb
there is only the stone that tells

the books he read.

Lit

Mister Shashlik wants to sleep the day off in the quiet rush of air conditioned soul. The habit of life gets old. No doubt. No imagination trying. On the last intersection to work he thinks of excuses for not working: infections, dead batteries, past lives, kids he's never heard of until now.

The light stiffens red, indifferent. That takes the noblesse out of it. He parks the junk Nova in a stony lot out of the way of the factory. Cold air strangles in grim oil and cigarettes wrap dirty remains of oxygen. A boarded up bar across the street is inhabited by nothing but garbage crows.

If he could turn, slouch on a laptop, look at excited pictures, the day could walk off without him. The other morning, the stringy guy who eats vendor sandwiches, plays euchre, and works the molding press said, "I'm gonna make an operator out of your ass easy." What should he say to get out of it? The last trip with his father they went east. Hudson River: and they saw the first human beings hit the strand. The sun invents their shadows; the people look like glowing shadows, an overused substance in everyone.

And he was going toward it, going toward a beautiful city.

Cinderella Hour

Mr. Judy was getting tucked down on to the bed
up in the tower. Gothic angles. Stark blond red brick
and razor wired silver loops ran along the heads
of the walls and guard towers. Half remember it tall,
gaunt Frankenstein castle, thundered and flashed—
don't know how I imagined an execution would be in
what memory now sees as a tower. I had no real idea
about such things. We were kept distant, sang songs,
an odd body of protestors in a lot fenced by cops,
a few neo-Nazis that came ill dressed for the cold.
We shivered, studied the prison view, imagined life
in leg irons, zebra suits with pickaxes and rocks—
a con in a bowler, a leg crossed over the other, tilted
like Pisa on an axe handle, a pinkie rooting his teeth
—scene from a Chaplin silent that never got made—
then the cell: the body prayed, showered, shaved.
A last meal: two lobster carcasses left untouched.

The Half of It

I

You can control these episodes with heavier medication. You can try more liquids, green vegetables and use very little salt. Or we can bore a hole through the bone behind your ear, drive a shunt up inside, and drain the pressure. If it becomes too much.

II

If in this river valley it's nearly spring. I went out into the cool washed day. So I wrote you. So what? I know I love it too much that Nerval said "to remember is to invent." The girl beside me twists a coil of hair around and inside itself. She's thin as rain writing the story about me. Her baggy green pants blossom, touching my thigh and the delicacy thereof. When Nerval saw a litho of himself, he scribbled on it, "Je suis l'autre". Can you imagine the way we're always living our movie. It's like a deeper dream that can't wake up from us. And still spring detonates its scent in the filthy vine beds. Is it sad to think? Who could understand when they came across him what led to a strangulation in the cold Paris alley where he was suspended, the closing chapters in his pockets. I have only the loose translation.

III

Nerval had his "mystic gates" above a courtyard. Incarcerated. In a whole other life—I met a woman in a pub, her face thronging shadows, softly visible in the bottled in bond smolder. "Sit here. Talk with me?" she said. The soft clutch of her hand is more important than anything I can say. I can point to the dramatic shift. But how to break the question in two? I don't know any more than you how to solve the hard simplicity of yes and no. Myself, I cannot see, apartment after apartment; this whole expanse I cannot breathe.

"O Christ! Look! The Horn of Africa! We can see it from the ledge of Gibraltar. The air salt and smoky. When the wild white horses drove off of the surf, I almost fainted." When she says we, I know it's him. I'm tired of being Judas, you do it awhile.

My slapstick despair gallops through me and into the blasting spray of sun. I was mostly scared from the moment I found my English teacher standing in a corner of the tall stage anteroom, weeping into a book. I promised myself I'd invent this half a kilometer of golden air and climate, here at the nullity of everything, the intersection of Harold and Alice. The signs are always stolen. I remember where they go.

IV

Dark gnarled shot up stop signs, houses in a dark stupor, all the ill-defined landscape. And here I dream of you for the first time after all this time. You were on a late night talk show, doing comedy, later swinging on an enormous thin drum suspended from the catwalks. Later in a car with my sister you tell me, “we can fuck all the time now, it’s ok.” I say nothing. Look into the palms of my hands.

The Tonight Show

Look at him again tonight,
bugged by his disappointed shtick,
the pulp and Gibran he loves like he loves

stolen, dying monologues,
ripped off bits of other men's jokes
told with bared upper teeth, a shaky,
bitten lower lip of a laugh
swiped from that late talk show host.

My father pilfers a fifth from the honorary
cylinder sleeve given when he retired
from Sealed Power where he dropped a quarter
years over a hone and ream, cutting
piston sleeves for engines: "Nothing
like making big machines work."

Evening against the pillars,
the systolic hours melt into
the yard's soaked cake, where we
drift to my car in the poised drive.

Magellanic clouds, vague giants bound:
too many ways for saying precisely nothing,
for how it works between us.

He put a bowl of milk to a kitten,
maybe the last thing I saw him do.

And something,
          something said I didn't get.

Like Roland's Horn

I

In those days rented him the air is smoke and fresh snow. Gone mornings to a factory; logs enough hours to fall shy of benefits and full time. Inside a papered window he studies the story and picture all over. An exploded shuttle coming to earth through a hole in a day ten years ago. Feeling oddly without history or weight, he soothes his hands in machine oil. buffs the resonant surface until he sees the room bent around the rowed horns on racks overhead. His friend's son is learning to play a French horn, an instrument he likes for the dangled coil and a name like pastry, the metal's melting buttery feel. Imagine the complicated wind it takes in the valves; the sympathy applied to its formation as it lies prone on the finishing table.

Spent evenings through streets,
music stores, lead to the deli where he eats.
A scared, cruel look appears from a window
in a house near the rails of the underpass
near where he secretly lives.
In winter light that weak arch looks
hardly a road through the bedding
where it seems it is pain after all
that holds its warmth in the fat coat of snow,
so safe it's a shame when you have to go
in early morning before traffic rises and
snowplows scrape drives clean,
and trucks salt the exhausted roads down.

II

Few clear lights on in houses.
What would it take to sleep?
A kindness that doesn't mind
the ditch the calm dark spreads
under his feet when it's too late to see.

III

Metallic weeds shiver along damp asphalt;
only the twenty feet of sky overhead.
Snow feels miraculous when it first falls.

Love and recombinant humanized anti-p185HER2 monoclonal antibody

No switch.
        The twisted bedding luminous gray,
I wipe my mouth off.
        Tall windows, large rooms.
                Panic Bird in the ward,
you beat your heart
on the wall,
the caged window,
all day the flood the fire
the winter pushing in.
                I swung the broom
        that knocked the lights out
                and killed the spider.

Arms and legs anchored to bed,
"death at work as you see bees behind a glass"
hive of her chest.
        I ask my sister if she's getting better;
she never looks better.
        Is this the way she wants?
Her pillow, her bed
                positioned to the light?

Last Ditch Apologia

I

We will never be vindicated, will we? If we were still twin in earthly terms there would always be the wrong gesture, the wrong shirt, the lip service we'd end up swearing. Only sometimes, I'm happy with a scent or shred of music, or I've had too much to drink. I'm sorry you're dead. But what does it matter when it was just us, when you're buried inside me, still drinking from the same famished tube. I hate what happiness I have in this ugly place, because in a way your car is always in the park where they found you, pointing at a tall golden tree trembling in milky sunlight across the heavy river I cannot look across.

II

The priest standing on a blown day, flying vestments above a hole in the ground, tells me you're in a heavenly country because you did not consent. But I knew as the first fists of dirt hit the lid that that was bullshit. All you are going to see is six feet of fucking dirt. Oh, I miss you. I wish you'd known one meaningful thing that could have saved you this freak hope of life, the memory of our ridiculous poverty, this familiar shame that wears us as a skin. If you were alive, like me you'd be on your knees beside your bed under a twenty-watt bulb, praying indifferent air for money so we could live in a nice house. I can't say if we were twins or a hallucination I made from myself.

III

Not even God with his knee on your chest, his voice of a million impassable rivers can pry open our secret life, can find the empty house at the edge of the field near our home that we pretend to strangers is where we live.

IV

I stare down brute headstones of the abandoned dead and swept sky, crouch inside the black dresses, the faltered line of trees. Between the stalled road and the fluttering crowd,

V

I cannot see a way to go.

I wish illusion had been enough to feed on, pictures in lovely warped old books we looked through; one with a shining Spanish girl, healthy, alive, hoisting her woven basket of red and green grapes, the sun tangible as melting butter on spilled hillsides, the staff and bridge of notes to a simple song floating beneath her that she must have been singing on her way somewhere. I can't tell you how these words taste in my mouth. If anything was, you were.
I wish I were with you.

Late Conversions

I wrote on J's bar tab, "I can't be yr famly," tell him under my breath it was just a thought.
I looked away from him at my friends swelling into a nearby booth, laughing together
at a joke I couldn't hear. His face seemed to blank, fold up, looked up with a vacant laugh,
then scribbled on the reverse a nervous line about a chimpanzee, a box, a banana.
I don't remember. He looked a little opened up then, like a Cornell box hung and glued.
So odd. It wasn't my fault. My father was coming from Virginia with his slab of venison
and his pulpit. Naomi was leaving for Cyprus to sculpt. Later we were all going to smoke
a brick and see the Foreign Film Stars. He was quiet. So was I. And here, the lemon butter
light melted over us. Later, he was talking ok. Got up. Went to the bar. Drank a shot.
Seemed to evaporate in front of us, waving stupidly from his warped smile. What he
vanished into, I couldn't say: sad voltages, wanton want not—the voice of Mahalia Jackson
falling through the wireless, "I'm gonna wait for my change to come …"

to the terminal,

every window sees through,
dispatched elsewhere, the horns of trains bloom,
the cars drag fuel, stock, pearls, miraculous drugs,
the tonnage of what god knows

could buy a new world
shifted in my vision so I never see any geography
but caved-in faces relentless with eyes, scored and overheard
breathing into withered letters "oh, love …"
piso mojado, bring the mop and bucket: it must all get old

with derelicts collecting against counters, bandaged
in scarves and hats,
dealt with bodies they can't operate

reread a prophetic ticket
relive stamped dates, the karmic transfer
as more than phenomena of days swallowing themselves:
got roads to burn, fuel to drive

an intercom, not the Lord, calling my names: *To—From—*

On Divine Sorrow

in pale ontic night
he has your name on his breath
city twilight swung
in tightrope wiring
from one building to another
where I first see myself
guarding a motel door
my family in suitcases,
in another strange city, god knows

I used to dream these things:
I'd find a job, bankroll a mansion,
cure what bad fate was doing us in

invent a truth we could weaponize
and save my little tribe from eviction,
laughter in the eyes we meet

I could levitate this stuff all night, take in
snow's sharp breath drawn through
the window's broken stare
the riot inside

I hear my father asleep
on the bed, moaning
sometimes when he starts
he can't stop himself

Letter to a Girl in Cokedale

I don't know a way to tell you your days
won't be shacks and trailers thrown
on the hill's back, where boom time

expired before you could get your hands
on it. The black cone of slag is from years
the town was stripped beneath its mantled

weather for what it had. What remains
are dwarfed rows, the stucco caves of families

dropping along the slope toward the school,
excavated like the boarding house
where unmarried miners used pulleys

to run their dirty clothes to the launderer,
their thin shirts in the stiff air
drifted as though they had slipped off

their skin and asked the caustic soap
to bleach the smut from the seams for good.
You can't buy yourself anything

in the mercantile that stands on the lower
drive, too derelict to trouble
with anything like a past. Who knows who

they were, the man and woman hung
in a post office niche, dressed up against
the trestle wall in a time it seemed too rich.

Days thrown to the fire as of no worth,
as if there were more to it than a vain
prospect of a miraculous face vanished

into the anonymous.

Rachel's Children

I know, we have the 911 replay,
Chatty news whose gospel verily

Insists there's a very real reason why
The accidentally dead for Christmas

Never call up from the depths of hours,
The charred sands and rice paddies,

Chance murders in sunlit schoolrooms.
Since in our soft wars all are equally

Good and dead. The governor for life
Sends guns and prayers for protection,

A handsome stone for children
Who sat pretty maids all in a row.

Pale green-eyed Jesus arose once,
rebuked winds and wild sea, didn't he?

The Will of Inanimate Things

Around the boarded house and the remains
of estate—how will they find the wreckage?
Grass wet, bristling underfoot, things will have their way
where birds wire nests in sockets up under the fascia,
in the guttering with plastic and grass shreds.
Weeds scribbled down the porch stoop.

Try to make something of it:
dripped garage eaves tap a stone step,
the pond across the road smokes, silvers,
bedded in shocks of sedge.

Let's take this day as evidence.
How many bodies and days have we known?
Mercury at autumn's rim
sees through the iced pane.

Muffled in a parka, he pulls out
his head from under the car's hood.
Somewhere off away a hammer barks
in the cold—tacks back in echo.

Home from whatever war it was this time,
you can't be sure what's coming at you—
what's coming to catch you from behind.
He kept re-upping until after the divorce.

Then he came home.
He made a bed in the dining room,
made a list—asked to be calm
he claimed to slow his heart down three beats
a minute. Nothing of war in life and sleep,
save the tremor in his lower lip.

Reintroducing the Wolf

I

How did you meet him?
In a room without walls, his face
a verdict peering from dirty
leaves that wept cold droplets.
His narrow jaw yawned, then
he sniffed the air.
His eyes hung gold
sharp staring out.
I felt him more than saw him
moving in my ribcage.
Afraid to breathe, I backed away.
Back into the hot light,
into the tarry lot of a pharmacy,
blinking—alone.

II

Where are you? Frozen aisles.
Hungry for what sounds good,
unused to making supper myself.
Our mother felt like a mother
with too many kits. Ribs sharpened,
my sister and I slept the day.

III

Bed of sand. Margins of a road.
Evening aloft, my sister drives
me home again. Listen.

IV

Where the ground steams,
where nothing goes by name,
the field's green hair is stayed.

Footfalls make a way.
Unbridled—quick force

without body, with no memory,
stepping up in to the dark.

Saint Francis Buys Time

This afternoon the sky's half-lit bad reproduction rolls on me. Outside the Laughing Planet café violet clouds revolve low and fast. I like it this way. Leaves shatter black in a wet wind, hover and collapse around a steeple down on the liquid street. Near me, a man teaches his son backgammon with a broken board and a podge of game pieces, discarding rules when they are too much to deal. Again, the ragged couple in red dreadlocks sit on the orange bench with a dirty paperback named *Super Tantric Sex Power* crumbling in their hands like burnt toast.

There are couples all the time. I envy their charmed bodies with a mixed bag of solace and regret that grows from the cavity of my heart. And then sometimes, I'd like to psychically disrupt relationships all over town, take them down unrelenting ways I've been, ways I'm going. Even though there's radiant chocolate and Melissa asking, "Have you moved into that house of yours yet?" I want to be dark tormented as a tower, a lion ringing its shining chains as it climbs.

I feel the vaporous rain. Sparrows flicker around my chair legs, bite pieces of cranberry and pecan off the cement. They look medieval, mechanical toys the way they hop and nod. Their small lives are larger than my own. For not the first time, I wish I could be a handsome life, a Bronte with strong black eyes and a penknife.

"I'm so tired of being a man." I want to walk down the street stripped of any vesture of what it means. I want the booklet, *On Being Human.* I would buy it. I want something that tells me, "You are a professional." I want to be in the dojo when a master presents me a black belt in quiet, loyal, and honorable.

If there's no understanding for me, I have no hope of you, and don't know from love. There's no one who tells me, "Now you get it." Except the scraggly plumber leaning against a bookshelf in a library with an *Atlas of Birds of the World* in his hand.

Instead, I'll swallow shadows, swollen wet roses, burgundy thorns, candy aspirin if it kills me. I have no cure for life. Like the child I still am, I thought, if it gets better that will be worse. I'm only spirit and spilled on the page, devoured by what I try to possess in one body, one soul. Enough of me. I don't know the half of it.

Wherever my words are, in my mouth, they are sour.

Alterwise by Earthlight

I'm sure I could have spent life elsewhere
in a basement apartment playing *Avalon*
up all night with my awful thoughts
in one of those choked out towns
that are low to earth and gray white lined
with one story houses whose owners
you will never see, and choicest pain,
yet ugly pretty in ways not many care for.
The opposite of me is you and that jazz.
The theory of me and you written
on underclass grade writing paper,
in my otherworldly online existence.
When I read medieval arts of rhetoric
I think of satanic devices:
the Iron Maiden of Truth—step inside the
tongue teaser; the pear of anguish, which
not even the ones who made it knew how
it was supposed to be used, the thumb
screws of brain entrainment. Blood
agency was maybe always the way that
oiled the gears of time and traffic.
I thought strappado was a poetic form,
the hell of the head's fear of desire.

The Opposition

Whoever had the first idea of sex wasn't
the eminent Jonny Skaggs and his Skaggisms.
Jonny Skaggs and his cycle pasted with Hello Kitties
telling me his wife doesn't believe in faithfulness.
San Antonio and the Riverwalk running with
Margarita and salt and piss and paper cups,
not a few streets away from the Alamo.
Biking past one of those white dead mansions
in that violet evening stewed in heat and lilacs,
I see a young man shooting up his arm
tourniqueted, vein popped, evening's blue heat
looking up at me with a friendly mouth,
a gooey smell in the air like pipe resin.
That night in the street's crush and bloom,
a fat man thuds an oil drum, raves his politics
as a drunk airman in uniform stupidly dances.
A woman with her man catches me staring at her,
unclasps her smile, throws her wink, makes me
immortal and infinitely lonesome.

Late Empire

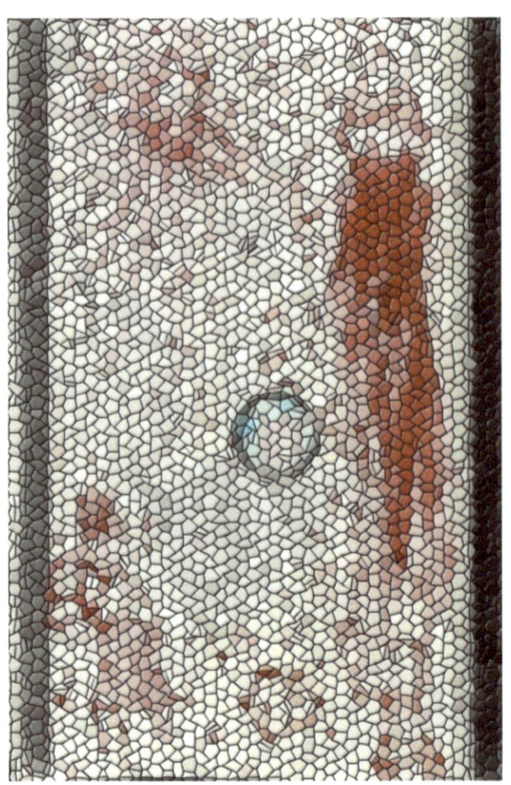

In the Cosmo bar across from the Empire State,
a thin man asks if she knows how serial killers kiss.
Drinks and voices float by in half-dark warmth,
its drunk citizens load up an angelic elevator
where someone will get murdered in the shaft.
He tells her, love is out of style, unmappable,
unlike DaVinci, weaknesses don't make an arch.
Arc of a meaning missed, there's no reversing
the way things turn out—you can't not become.
When she looks over at a table with three women
their faces glow smooth and soft as children's.
With every move there is an equal and opposite.
By the time she makes it down to the ground floor,
to the front seat of his car, she is hit with a spell,
her heart lost any reservation and she thinks
the street should now express unspeakable repose.

"One on the left cheek for him, one on the right for you,
and one on the forehead. For control."

Life Behind the Nylon Curtain

No one has it that bad in the blue town.
Nylon curtains wake white windows
in the upper room of that house passed
on the way to work, like someone forgot
their sleep the night before and now dawn
readies to crack a 4 a.m. sky whose air
ices through the scarved mouth down
where all the love and trouble lies warm
at the chest's core congealed with
tetrachloroethylene and metal dust
from the grinding machine in shop
that may allow to not quite feel
the tin moon in a tree's black forks
shiver the piecrust snow on walks
that follow me around and round
glazed lawn's silver glass needles,
yet not one good witness to morning,
a seldom car crackling a far highway
that runs its bright horn through
whatever now feels so sure under
slow smoke stacked cumulonimbus
tumble, loosed to night locked city
air and gated lengths only to flower
in gasoline and tar's thin, harsh drift
that laces pine's icy sweetness and
shivers the corroded horizon's brim
where a train's horn blooms and fails
over the still warm bodies of mute houses,
and steel-toed boots kill those starry flakes,
steps too slight to know if anyone's there.

Topping Off

From the bottom dark of the bunk beneath me
he asked what it's like to kiss a man. Drunk,
dizzy patterns of leaves troubled the block wall
and too weak to say, I told him what he wanted,
would believe: gigantic, not a little like being
swallowed alive by a volcano

a kick in the brain or hot gulp of cognac glowing
down the lungs as you get inside its warmth.
Wanted from head on down through flying dark,
what it was to be the thing wanted right then,
the swift bang of lit hash oil that all but kills you.

Not that anyone's pleading mouth serves
because then it never was mean and difficult to
kill a promise richer in telling than life, say what
no one wanted to know in the first place, the last
place you would find yourself alone. Taste,
though it feels wounded, torn out of itself, grows
indifferent because what is one more when you
had too many to begin with.

Prayer for My Daughter

As much to say she isn't going to paint a Vermeer any day soon
in that frame where I picture her, put meanings in her mouth. It
isn't about the photograph is it—there is more than this mute
hairbrush microphone, a clichéd cliché even for me?

In looking back, Vermeer's "Pearl Earring with a Girl"
or "Head of a Girl in a Turban" is the vintage equivalent
to "Girls Gone Mona Lisa" in *Waiting to Happen.*
I could leave out the theoretical parts of learned desire,
the look that looks you and can't unlock its gaze from
"look who she grew up to be"—a greyhound lean model
in a black leotard, her body's book and lure—colorless
as our lawless dreams—maybe I don't get details right
and these awful meanings, memory's lossy compression,
are more than ads for the need you need to need
a schooled look that turns our eyes stone,
our bodies to candy—the secret inside the secret
everyone desperately wants not desperately to see
and that we're told we won't unsee.

I can live without being shown you are the thing men want
when men want things—when you are more than the study of a
girl, not void of desire and not Barbie in a burqa
for every Xerox Apollo who will only turn you into a tree
or calls you Fred for fun after I spent all that time finding
a name for you and only called you girl two weeks after
you were born but more than any words I wrap you in, that
pretend speak you—get a real microphone: "kick out the jams
(motherfucker)," Patti Smith's version of "Gloria", Hole's *Live
Through This.* Get a way to see through a planet full of eyes
within eyes, speak volumes in substance and form, shape the
lyric dirt at the dark and shining core of it all—my fearless one
—go tear the world down.

Come Again

I'm about to turn nine when
I nearly drown in Lake Manitou,
will never now learn to swim.
My uncle owns a smoke shop
where they carry me in towels
away from faces and voices
into the dark heat, his rough hands
pressing life back into me.
The earth smells like sour tears.
the low income, the unwashed
light in the cool sprawl of dusk,
burning trash and fresh fruit
seeps in a screen window
he never closes. To me it is here.
There in beauty, in the lostness of it.
At the edge of a river, my pale life,
from earth to air, pulled from the water.

Herald

He walks up to the light and spies
a military poster flap on a guardrail,

an icy moon's broken tooth on the crags
of churches out beside interstates,

to a stairwell behind a used car lot
that leads down to a bedroll and a tarp

while across the street a man eats
a fat sandwich in a garish deli,

a girl strolls a baby in a shopping cart.
People are streets he can't drive.

He feels the pressure of voices,
not the sounds but their pressure,

turns around to me, his hands
on either side of his head and shouts,

"Can't you hear that black sunlight."

In the Region of Ice

Harry J. Johnson

Monday, Autust 18, 1969

Harry J. JOHNSON, 46, formerly of Rochester, was killed Friday at 5 p.m. in an accident at his home, 504 West Jackson street, Mentone. Mr. Johnson had jacked up his auto and had just begn to work under the front end when the vehicle slipped off the jack and crushed him.
Born July 22, 1923, at North Liberty, he was the son of John and Beatrice BECK JOHNSON and had lived in Mentone the past four years, moving from Rochester. His marriage was in 1960 at Rochester to Mary Frances KELLY, who survives.

The Frigid Imperial™ *casket lowering device* has become a favorite among customers because of its quality of construction and its assurance of performance.

I want to explain myself. Not myself exactly, but what happened the spring I found the baby skunk behind the empty milk house, dying, or what I took to be dying, in the muddy hollow of a cow's deep hoof print. I found the fist-size baby with its half closed eyes, rocking slowly side to side, moving with an interior music I couldn't. Unsettled weather hovered over us, warm at noon and cold in the evening, patched light, a weather I stupidly called in my school notebook, "the weather of disillusion." Always a blue-black thunder bank along the windy, shining green back of a hill, and after the storms washed through, it felt cold from the inside out. Saber grass, cattails idle along the stiff surface of the irrigation pond, disturbed only with muskrats wrapped in slick dirty wet coats like someone's henchmen waiting for a murder in the clay bank hovels underneath cool glasshouse sky.

I'm not in school. I stay inside listening to Patti Smith's "Birdland" all the time. My room, school, the world wide seems all one heavy metal melody anyway. One of my brothers-in-law died a few days before; crushed by a car he was working on in his backyard. A big round man, half-Navajo, who smoked squat cigars and drove trucks. He acted fatherly with me, though in an odd, disinterested way. Like giving me an adult bike but never teaching me how to ride it. Maybe he didn't want to take my father's place. Maybe not let on he wanted a son. He would invite me out to his place by having my sister ask me. Mostly, in his house, smelling sweet coffee and oranges, I watch cartoons or go outside, climb up and cradle down in the hot, sumptuous haymow.

But what I was saying. Each print looked sculpted out like a badly thrown pot, narrow tall bowls that hadn't been fired. Leaning down to the muddy cup that perfectly fit the baby, there were no tracks of small feet, no way to see how it had gotten into the funnel. Like a god, a Pan, placed its godly foot, then laid the creature off its palm inside the depression for its immaculate abandonment.

Deep, fresh prints pocket the whole space of the paddock, as though animals struggled and sunk even deeper trying to walk out of it. There were no cattle on the farm where we rented the house, and no reason or way someone else would bring them on to the farm. I couldn't understand where the prints had come from or why anyone would have led a small heard into a fenced enclosure. The cinderblock house was oblong, obscene weeds and fat, pink flowers, small windows dull white, fogged with dirt, and inside. There were no feed stations, no milking equipment, only the abandoned steel tank in a separate chamber, a smaller, cheaper kind with a yellow ball float in a bell jar to measure tank volume; scabbed and chipped holding stalls whose locking gates swung and clang like jail doors. The tall cement walkway where the holding stalls, almost the same smooth wall like stone as the chamber they lowered Harry's casket into with gold poles of a lowering device called a frigid casket stand, his box thronging with starburst chrysanthemums and a red, gold lettered banner that sailed, *Devoted Husband – Loving Father.*

Later there are the kind shadows and rooms and movements; long drawn cars and people discharged from them that in memory now are all one shapeless tone, the simplified moment that tastes like the kinds of food people offer at receptions for the dead: "I'm sorry he's dead. I don't understand … have some strawberry ice cream?"

I wanted to touch it, though it looked sick and weak. I would have picked it up if I had gloves or tongs. I felt I should be able to do something, but those were abstract days, and prone to lose myself in myself. I got off my dirty knees and took the memory, as if it would be enough to save the small creature in my head.

Free Admission

He puts on the radio in the next room. The house got too old to have doors and heat,
so the upper rooms freeze,
obscure with ruined odors you can't name or put out of your mind. You won't sleep.
Each semi-quaver a feather the weight of fear

as he's lying pressed close enough to the pitted wall to eavesdrop for whatever
warped ache in the vinyl brings from the radio's crackling riff.
Doubtless he wants to turn off his molecules, dissolve old ridicule in dreams.

Dreams are not dreams at all—more sharks, dirty water,
a shuddering flux that won't shear
off or fix, no matter you want to break the law

our life foretells and love disobeys: nothing faster than light. Nothing
how you're unwelcomed to a party, but loved by the godlike rush
hymning in the blue circuitries, the lavish waves shimmering off cymbals,

the drummed crush in your ears in the back dark
of a backseat whose cocked guitar wows and flutters pretty ecstasy: the vintage diver
drowned in stuttering movies that kick him free

of loss, lose him where there's nothing. Where there is nothing, there is blues
transfusion, the muddied waters like a twilight episode.
He didn't say he knew they invited him for fun, for a joke to get drunk—listen to him

get off on sad family, happy to slug at a bottle of clear syrup for vodka.
Admit: sob, undress, and pour him all night into anyone's hand. This must feel good to him,
nearly friendly their erect lips and eyes as cameras,

going for that liquid feeling that feels divine. His soul striptease must be a riot
giggling inside him, getting sick

on the abrupt drop. That sting along the mouth's edges doesn't ever leave, and what
screw turns him must turn me, unasked, or knot
twisting—you can't tell anyone else.

Rehearsal

She must have thought she was working for the fire department
in the city of Troy, and uptown, cloud-rapt Achilles with all his spectral armies,
sulking in the cell of his chest too disheartened to slaughter anyone.
Cassandra only, blundering down stone streets fogged in hot smoke and silhouettes,
tries to ascend a way out where mountains go abrupt to sky
from a valley floor. This looks like the way. I really don't recall myself.
I only look back down into it, pointing, and she was soaked in fire,
smoking, only say, "I'm from there."

The city gazed up.
Now, mired between thin wood and icy fields,
a stiff bed of firewood, hand on a strafed GMC instead of the chariot rein,
faded door lettered: Erie Lackawanna Railyard. I turn my head in memory,
in the crosswalk in a city I lived in once, where, sky's industrial flak and spring,
a woman drove past, all her children's arms and heads hung from the station wagon holes,
huffing exhaust, its door hardly wired shut with a twisted up coat hanger, crawling
to a bloodshot sign.

Winter in Tehran

O beautiful Allah, or whatever your name today,

why aren't the jet fighters in the air?

Fraying clouds that dock the Damavand,
that tooths the sky amid flats, lift my eyes

off the gazing asphalt under an overlook.
Gilgamesh, ancient fortitude, waiting time to end

all over again, for everyone to come home
from whatever Gitmo it is this time. My hand can't stay

any dawn that storms down on us.

Our daughter fogs a heart on the sliding door
of the fourth floor. Snow pack on black cypress

in the lot, jangled keys stick the lock, ignite hasty
prophecies, little fortellings for what I imagine will come

from all this imagining. Cold cracking lively
as even the bleat of the keyless fob may signal

should the car door come off—heartthudcarbomb.
As darling adoration for my only daughter,

I make a prayer with infinite draw weight shot through heaven
from the bunker of my reinforced soul, in the valley of my joy

and despair. As my safety catch,

as my deliverer, as a friend, as a known enemy,
are you getting this or not?

Sun and Air

The heart's sold to the movies. The roles and visions you haven't become.
Some will find you a stranded dog, name you what comes to hand. You will either not know or not feel to touch your body in the world. You are air and all you risk is a look.

Morning fiery and soaked, the sun again unasked, the pond's mirror mirror corridor, antes up, doubling. The rural route his mother calls Athens Road, forth and forth from a tar house to school. Let's make this simple. Pull from bed to make a foggy, dawn bus hours before anyone else has to. This room isn't new, wallpapered with maps cut from a gnarled atlas, no less a hangover without the buzz. If you get this far, there's a laugh for when you crash downstairs.

In class, the window buzzed with spring and flight, a teacher scowls at the Melville report, slaps down a stack of papers on his desk with a smack, groans, "Oh for godsake!", when you fail to say the sun in Chapter CXVIII is god watching.

The world cannot hear you. The world cannot hear you.

This world cannot.

Realism in Orange County

Should night turn inside out, and
lurk rooms for an unwedded hand,
let me show you around.

Glad you should make it this late
to the unscripted outskirts' dry hills,
windy eucalyptus. Glad to free

yourself from careless thoughts
in the hall that wasn't swept a year
seconds after it fall off my shoeshine,

a light that wasn't fixed since dawn;
sparrows cracking up
on the window's illusionary purchase,

friends who live with each other
to save rent and wander, love-like
streaming from the waist, the mind

barking madly at a bell like someone
took a cruel toy from its mouth,
set if off again, a meaness to anything

you think to say that argues at you
while you pull your coat on.
Key the lock, go hello this evening

lowered moon on guard at the walled in
night. Chorizo and mimosa, lure me
down in darling dark to your silver lighter,

glossy cigarette pack left aside the chaise,
an overlit pool's motionless sound.

4th Arrangement

There's room for anyone left to think,
whatever life is next in line,
chokes a Gauloise, plugs live rounds in the ceiling
from his Paris bathtub. A chair seated at a window
to the street, ride the idea of rain's icy spring,
going this far, no measure of the view. A room
with a bed, roughed up and in dire need of itself,
airless, no radio contact, hardly furnished
but cheap to live. You're welcome. Stay
as long as you like. Carpeted walls are worn
and warm and you can come and go when you want.
Think what it must have been then. Drink at hand.
A book and two fallen from sleep from a good bed.
A table by the tub with a light and an ashtray, half-eaten
apple caramelizing a page of Bruckheimer's Tragedies
to look down the well of time and see yourself surface.

Amenities

When down to Brighton, always the look of rain.
Only lately streets moan through the walls,
shaken rugs cracking, clicked lock, toy car siren—
then nothing much more. Nothing left under the door.
Eyeholes line hallways making out someone
with their head shut off. Breathe late blue snow
from the terrace that offers morning's sour

sweet. Windows through walls, thrilled
to make something of it: honeyed sweat, crackling
skillets, private cries, the headline squall headlong
along the floor, this morning's look off the watery
hours drowsed on the brain's infinite climate.

The lame pier half out to meet a nude sky,
in afternoon heady shore's tried expression.
Can't lose the weather, considering the intent,

ancient wing off an Icarus, that bit of wax,
all that said that won't hold, have what we have

to want to have on a cold, solitary beach
where we should go unclaimed, and nothing
can claim to find us.

Morning Shift

I pass the same house to work every day
where a warm family of four holds up
and think what the ticking, peaceable
dark kitchen waits for them to wake
must be like with its servitude and polite
white cups hooked up in the cupboard,
bedrooms that never heard a dirty word,
the almost hot layers of scented covers,
night over them calm as a windless pond.
And it's 4 a.m. now and then a car
grinds the icy highway, tears across the air
in half like the torn off adhesive strip
I dressed my fat red thumb up in
after it got crushed in an entry door.
I see a giant world, myself underneath,
even at that hour the world smells
like burning leaves and faintly of oil.
Moon snarled in a cold black tree
polishes snow sleeping on lawns
and walks beside soundless street.
Always I'm going to quit this job,
buy my way up to the Northwest
and find myself an Idaho homestead,
up near Salmon River, stockpile silver
dollars in a shoebox and live off Ramen,
whatever I can filch from a dumpster.
With no one's help live that way
until someone rings me up and says
we seriously need you down here.

Minor Portrait

It is in the airy skirting, a shivering dress
I bought her off the rack in a Goodwill
she'll remember this pale ache, a phone
ringing for months, filling in the winter sky,
I can no longer separate from my skin
as though everyone should feel and recognize
through my touch the tremor through all hours, struck with
a careful anger I was not to allow in front of anyone,
nor anything, having no choice to live apart
from my daughters, who may now be falling
to sleep, perhaps not in Kyoto or London depths,
and not gone, but just as good.

What I memorize precisely is missing,
is as strong as what I attempt to disregard,:
sporadic pulse in the lamp where she read
Alice even to the end, looking up startled,
elated, as though I'm already the phantom
extremity she will try to verify, like a mystic
trail of burnt dinner wandering upstairs
with my voice on days when I have custody,
the pink and white plastic record player cued
to glide her back down the house,
up into my arms with the big sweep out
into the yard and back, a sketchy waltz,
the neighbors pissed we've escaped gravity,
into the center of the street, she haunts
with joy, buoyant going out to the edge
into the weightless core where I exist
with her, altogether inseparable in my breath,
my absent profession.

Western Approaches
(On an Ancient Theme)

Before you can wake up, I sat the table with three.
One for you. Two for the girls asleep upstairs.
Pack myself in the same bedroom where I first touched you,
asked where you'd like the crib,
threw *300 Years of Chinese Poetry* against the wall.

My head against the door,
I think: Princess Wen-chi was captive of the Xiongnu
for twelve years, bore their ruler two daughters.
Then she was ransomed, having to leave her children behind,
her captor, the stone and scrubbed desert.

There's a place in that narrative painting,
the poem, when she must choose
the approaching cloud of rescue—

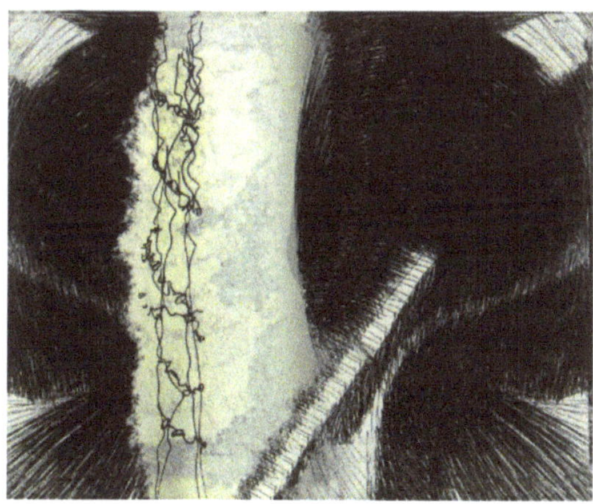

her nomad babies behind her
asleep in the tent staked on the blown steppes.
She cannot have both. She cannot have both,

though she stops, pitched mid-scene,
a riveted arrow, looking south; cut root of her.
Days found themselves in her hands,
a compass without cardinal points.
She never dyed herself with her grief,
stripped of all home and kingdom.

I want to call her up. Tell her, leave it with me.
You don't have to go through with this.

Feel the panel unfold the next scene
that will take you as it takes me.

"My daughters, my shadows, don't ..."

The Drunken Pugilist

Neat, clean shaven, sober moon.
Glassy sky as though to collect the day like
a sack of objects that in them reveal incipient
yet almost motionless night.

Winter's hooded light feels shadowed at noon
across the polar reach of north country,
that itself looks through you and holds light
helpless to lift much above fenced horizon,
boxed up farmland with cornfields, chunks
of ashen woods outlying the tin cup towns,
though night is radiant blackness miles deep
that packs the air so tight a cracked stick echoes
across what is left of this Christendom,
the stale, rented house lived with.

No holy solitude, or any other name of life.
Unexplored, unripe, seldom, apparently, present
to yourself you love the least useful things most
in the world, like it could explain an old hurt
that has nothing to do with your body.
As you move through strangers, friends,
or the most intimate rooms, your face is lost,
others become your arms and legs, hands and feet.

Crows flower the gothic chestnut beside the lake
ribbed with cattails and milkweed. The air smells blue
and cold but you are only ever in your own eyes.
The drunken pugilist wrestles his tongue.

I'm getting to my own dark now, a thing no one
will have any wild tears for.

To The Management

Always blackberries near a fence
that runs aside the woods,

it's this wire hanger that withholds
the field from the wild revenant

few too slight to feed,
straggled wiring, unowned

wood with no house except fresh low,
domed in snow, locust's fearlessly thorned

chambers. Handsome for its igloo
thicket's angry cuneiform stitch.

There is that occurrence.
Near empty day, winter shod,

here storm, come inside me,
almost say what's certain:

not sure it was winter or an aberrant
storm near spring that levied

a realm of snow on the wood's spine
and nowhere else—sun's neon gilt

all over, too low and far to warm
random wood, as if light issued

from the wood itself—cast through
a keyhole onto the going dream.

Dreams like arguments, try not trying
to try out for nonexistent lives

that have no origin, no arrival.

L. Heywood 2016

www.ingramcontent.com/pod-product-compliance
Lightning Source LLC
Chambersburg PA
CBHW041929010726
47507CB00003BA/228

9781946606020